Also available in the ORSON'S FARM™ series:

THE GREAT CHRISTMAS CONTEST
LET'S PLAY BALL!
THE BIG CAMP-OUT

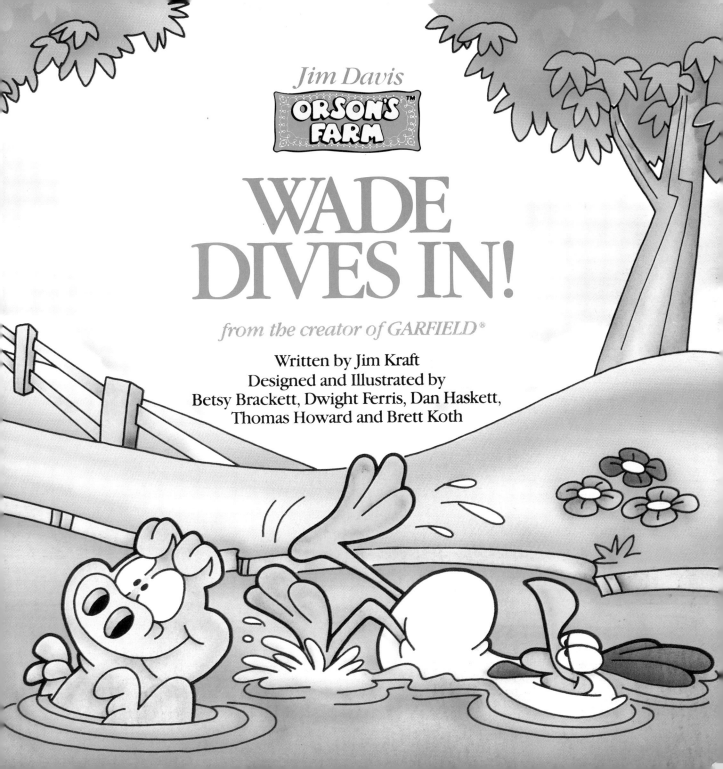

Jim Davis

ORSON'S FARM

WADE DIVES IN!

from the creator of GARFIELD®

Written by Jim Kraft

Designed and Illustrated by
Betsy Brackett, Dwight Ferris, Dan Haskett,
Thomas Howard and Brett Koth

A blazing summer sun baked the barnyard at Orson's Farm.

"It's so hot my comb is wilting," moaned Roy.

"I'm roasting inside this wool suit," gasped Lanolin.

"Even the worms are sweating," observed Booker.

"There's only one way to beat this heat," said Orson. "Last one into the pond is a rotten egg!"

"Hey! I resent that!" replied Sheldon.

"Sorry, Sheldon," said Orson. "I meant, 'Let's go swimming!'"

Orson, Roy, Bo, Lanolin, Booker, and Sheldon were soon splashing happily in the pond. But Wade was still standing on the bank.

"Dive in, Wade!" said Booker.

"No way!" replied Wade, trembling. "I'm afraid of water."

"Why are you afraid of water?" asked Bo.

"Because I'm afraid of EVERYTHING!"

Early the next day Wade went looking for Orson. He found Orson in the wallow, taking his morning mud bath.

"Orson, you've got to help me," said Wade.

"Let me guess," replied Orson. "You're afraid that space aliens are chasing you, right?"

"Wrong!" said Wade. "Tomorrow is my day to be afraid of space aliens. Today I want you to help me overcome my fear of water. Will you do it?"

"I'll try," said Orson. "But first I've got to slap some more mud behind my ears."

Orson decided that they had better start slowly. So he took an eyedropper and filled it with a little water.

"Now, don't be afraid," Orson said to Wade. "I'm only going to drip a single drop of water onto your bill."

"I can't watch," said Wade.

Orson squeezed the drop onto Wade's bill.
"Did you do it?" asked Wade.
"Yes," said Orson.
"That's what I was afraid of," said Wade.
"AAAAAAH! Help! Help! I'm drowning!" he
shrieked as he ran away.
This is going to be tough, thought Orson.

"Time for lesson number two," Orson said to Wade. "Try standing in this puddle."

"It looks awfully dangerous," observed Wade, "especially for a sinker like me."

"Don't be ridiculous," replied Orson. "That puddle can't be more than two inches deep. Now, hop in!"

Wade finally agreed to try. He jumped into the puddle . . . and immediately sank out of sight!

"You really *are* a sinker," said Orson, pulling him out. "How do you ever take a bath?"

"With a little water and a lot of screaming," gasped Wade.

Orson decided that they might as well practice in the pond. Roy and Booker came along to help.

"Jump in and I'll catch you," Orson instructed Wade. "Once you learn to float, everything will be fine."

Wade trembled all over.

"You can do it, Wade," called Booker. "Don't be afraid!"

"What's there to be afraid of?" added Roy. "Just watch out for the pond sharks and giant tidal waves."

"Sharks! Tidal Waves?" Wade nearly fainted.

"Some help you are, Roy," said Orson.

Wade finally managed to stop shaking.
"All right, I'm going to do it," he announced.
"I'm going to get a running start and dive into
this pond!"

Wade retreated fifty yards and tightened his inner tube. He raced toward the pond, hit the edge of the bank, started his dive . . .

"Go, Wade, go!" cheered Orson and Booker.

. . . and then he froze, practically in midair!
Orson, Roy, and Booker were amazed.
"How do you do that?" wondered Booker.
"Fear does strange things to your body,"
explained Wade.
"This duck is hopeless," said Roy.

When Sheldon went for a swim that afternoon, he discovered Wade sitting beside the pond.

"You look sad," said Sheldon.

"I'll never get over this fear," moped Wade. "I'm going to be a duck out of water for the rest of my life."

"Most of us are afraid of something," replied Sheldon. "I'm afraid to come out of my shell."

"I'm afraid that space aliens will take over my body and make me wear a watermelon on my head," said Wade.

"Wade, you need help," advised Sheldon.

Sheldon leaped into the water and began to kick his way across the pond. Suddenly, he got a cramp in his leg.

"Wade! Help! I'm sinking!" cried Sheldon.

"AAAAAAH!" shouted Wade. "What should I do?
What should I do? Help! HELP!"

Wade snatched up a long stick and held it out towards the little egg. "Here, Sheldon. Grab this!" he said.

"Grab it with what, you dopey duck!" sputtered Sheldon.

"Sorry, I forgot," said Wade.

Thinking quickly, Wade pulled out a straw, stuck it in the pond, and began to suck up the water.

Unfortunately, there was more water than Wade could suck up!

"Will you stop fooling around and save me?" yelled Sheldon.

There's only one thing to do, Wade told himself. I've got to dive into the water and rescue Sheldon. I've got to do it!

Wade teetered on the edge of the pond. "Hang on, Sheldon! I'm coming!" he cried. "Just keep an eye out for pond sharks!" Wade closed his eyes tightly and dived in!

The next few minutes were filled with lots of thrashing and splashing. Sometimes Wade seemed to be rescuing Sheldon. Sometimes Sheldon seemed to be rescuing Wade.

Finally Wade was able to shove Sheldon onto
the bank, just as Orson, Roy, and Booker raced up.

"What happened?" Booker asked anxiously.
"I got a cramp," explained Sheldon. "And
Wade—*cough, cough*—jumped in and saved
me."

"Wade, you did it?" cried Orson, "You overcame your fear of water!"

"I did?" said Wade.

"You're standing in it, Nutso," said Roy.

"I am? said Wade. He looked down at his submerged feet. "Hey! I am!"

The following day Wade was about to try
another dive, when Orson suddenly surfaced.
   Wade took one look at Orson and shrieked,
"Space alien! Space alien! AAAAAAH!"
   Orson laughed. "I guess you can't overcome
all your fears in one day," he said. "especially if
you're afraid of EVERYTHING!"